To PEYTON AND GIANNA,

MERRY CHRISTMAS 2017

Love,

Grandma & Grandpa

ALWAYS THANKFUL FOR YOU!

Cover image: Donald Wallace
Cover design: Michael Barrett

This book is printed on acid-free paper. ♾
Copyright © 2016 by Jon Gordon. All rights reserved.

Published by John Wiley & Sons, Inc., Hoboken, New Jersey.
Published simultaneously in Canada.

For general information about our other products and services, please contact our Customer Care Department within the United States at (800) 762-2974, outside the United States at (317) 572-3993 or fax (317) 572-4002.

Wiley publishes in a variety of print and electronic formats and by print-on-demand. Some material included with standard print versions of this book may not be included in e-books or in print-on-demand. If this book refers to media such as a CD or DVD that is not included in the version you purchased, you may download this material at http://booksupport.wiley.com. For more information about Wiley products, visit www.wiley.com.

ISBN 978-1-118-98691-2 (cloth): ISBN 978-1-118-98694-3 (ebk); ISBN 978-1-118-98695-0 (ebk)

Printed in the United States of America

10 9 8 7 6 5 4 3 2 1

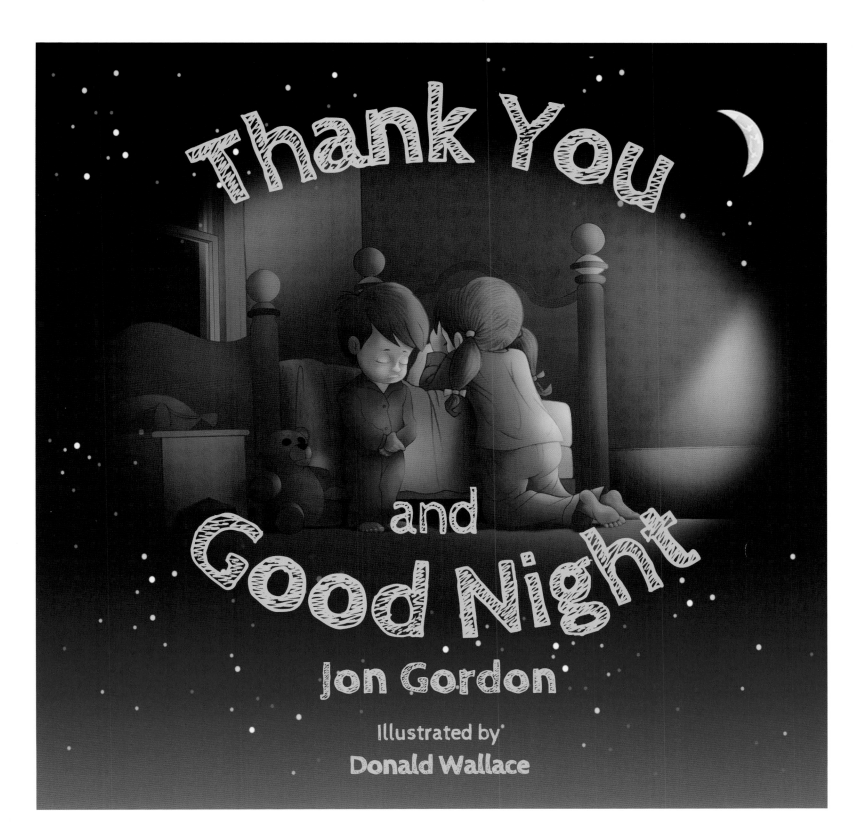

Thank You

and

Good Night

Jon Gordon

Illustrated by
Donald Wallace

WILEY

Thank you for this day...

Thank you for this night...

Thank you for the sun...

that shines so bright.

Thank you for butterflies...

and ladybugs.

Thank you for grandmas
and grandpas...

who give great big hugs.

Thank you for Fridays, Sundays...
and all the days of the week.

Thank you for games
like tag, kickball...

and hide-and-go-seek.

Thank you for bunnies, puppies...
and my teddy bear.

Thank you for joy, happiness...
and family who care.

Thank you for my brain,

       and eyes that wink.

And don't forget smelly feet that stink!

Thank you for smiles,

and jokes that are funny.

Thank you for flowers,
and bees that make honey.

Thank you for horses
and cows that go moooo.

Thank you for kitty cats

and dogs that go poo. (Ewwww!)

Thank you for happy thoughts

and sweet dreams,

thank you for 11 flavors

of my favorite ice creams.

Apples, oranges, and blueberries too...

Band-aids, love, and kisses

that heal my boo-boo.

Thank you for the love
        that wipes away my troubles,

thank you for my warm bath and bubbles.

Thank you for the words

They're so easy to say.

Thank you for the gifts and blessings...

we receive each day.

So thank you for my blanket,
thank you for my bed,

thank you for this pillow
that rests my tired head.

It's time to go to sleep...

and turn off the light...

Thank you God for everything...

Thank You and Good Night.